Dear Parent:
Your child's love of reading starts here!

Every child learns to read in a different way and at his or her own speed. Some go back and forth between reading levels and read favorite books again and again. Others read through each level in order. You can help your young reader improve and become more confident by encouraging his or her own interests and abilities. From books your child reads with you to the first books he or she reads alone, there are I Can Read Books for every stage of reading:

SHARED READING
Basic language, word repetition, and whimsical illustrations, ideal for sharing with your emergent reader

BEGINNING READING
Short sentences, familiar words, and simple concepts for children eager to read on their own

READING WITH HELP
Engaging stories, longer sentences, and language play for developing readers

READING ALONE
Complex plots, challenging vocabulary, and high-interest topics for the independent reader

ADVANCED READING
Short paragraphs, chapters, and exciting themes for the perfect bridge to chapter books

I Can Read Books have introduced children to the joy of reading since 1957. Featuring award-winning authors and illustrators and a fabulous cast of beloved characters, I Can Read Books set the standard for beginning readers.

A lifetime of discovery begins with the magical words "I Can Read!"

Visit www.icanread.com for information
on enriching your child's reading experience.

The Littlest Leaguer Copyright © 1976, 2008 by Syd Hoff All rights reserved. No part of this book may be used or reproduced in any manner whatsoever without written permission except in the case of brief quotations embodied in critical articles and reviews. Printed in the United States of America. For information address HarperCollins Children's Books, a division of HarperCollins Publishers, 1350 Avenue of the Americas, New York, NY 10019. www.harpercollinschildrens.com

Library of Congress Cataloging-in-Publication Data is available.

ISBN-10: 0-06-053772-8 (trade bdg.) — ISBN-13: 978-0-06-053772-2 (trade bdg.)

ISBN-10: 0-06-053773-6 (lib. bdg.) — ISBN-13: 978-0-06-053773-9 (lib. bdg.)

1 2 3 4 5 6 7 8 9 10   ❖   First Edition

THE LITTLEST LEAGUER

Story and pictures by
Syd Hoff

HarperCollinsPublishers

Of all the players in

the little league,

Harold was the littlest.

"Maybe you ought to go home
and come back next year,"
said Shirley the shortstop.

6

"Maybe you ought to go home
and not come back at all,"
said Big Leon, who played first base
because he had such a long reach.

This only made Harold try harder.

He tried in the infield,

but ground balls did not

have to take much of a hop

to go over his head.

He tried in the outfield,

but the other outfielders

had longer legs and could move

under a fly ball faster.

Harold tried to make up for all this
as a hitter, but there seemed to be
no bat light enough for him
and balls zoomed past him
before he could swing.

"Please don't feel badly,
but I'm afraid there's only one place
I can put you,"
said Mr. Lombardo the coach.

He put Harold on the bench.

Harold sat there,

game after game,

wearing out the seat of his pants.

Sometimes he took care of
the team's bats.

Sometimes he brought them
cold drinks.

"I'm tired of being so little,"
thought Harold,
and he stayed out in the rain
when a game was stopped,
hoping it would make him grow
like the flowers.

All it did was make him wet.

"Maybe you ought to try
eating green vegetables," said Shirley
when the team went home.
"Better still, try forgetting
where we play," said Big Leon.

17

That night Mr. Lombardo came
to Harold's house.
He knew his littlest leaguer
needed cheering up.

18

"You're letting your size bother you.
There have been
many great baseball players
who were not tall," said the coach.
And Harold's father agreed with him.

The two men talked about
short players who were
in the Baseball Hall of Fame,
and Harold listened
until he had to go to sleep.

So Harold kept sitting on the bench,

game after game,

until it was the last game

of the season.

The winner of this game would be

the Little League Champions.

The score was nothing to nothing.

Harold watched Shirley
catching line drives and
making great plays at shortstop.
But in the top of the third
the score was still
nothing to nothing.

He watched Big Leon

using his long reach to take throws

from all over the infield

and get runners out at first base.

But in the top of the seventh

the score was still

nothing to nothing.

"Oh, if I could only help them,
really help them," thought Harold,
as his team came in
to take their final turn at bat
in the last half of the ninth inning.

"Move over," said Big Leon,

shoving him off the bench.

Harold sat on the ground knowing

he didn't deserve to sit with the team.

He just kept sitting there,

thinking of all those short players

in the Baseball Hall of Fame.

Then with two out,

the next three batters got infield hits

and Harold's team

had the bases loaded.

"Ow-www!" cried a voice.

It was Big Leon

getting ready to bat.

He had stepped in a hole

and twisted his foot.

"I can't walk on it,
I can't even stand on it,"
said Big Leon as they helped him
back to the bench.

29

"Harold, it's up to you now.

We need a hit to win.

The bases are loaded

and all our pinch hitters are sick

from too many cold drinks.

Will you please go to bat for us?"

asked Mr. Lombardo.

Harold walked to the plate.

He stood as tall as possible,

hoping to scare the pitcher.

But Knuckles Smith,

the opposing pitcher,

threw a fast ball

right across the plate.

"Strike one!"

shouted the umpire.

Knuckles wound up

and pitched again.

This time he threw his curve.

"Strike two!"

shouted the umpire.

On the bench, Harold's team groaned.

Some of them got ready to leave.

"It's all over," said Big Leon.

Then Harold got an idea.

He crouched at the plate

as small as possible.

He crouched so low,

and became so small,

that Knuckles could not find

the strike zone.

The next pitch came
towards the plate,
but it was too high.
"Ball one!" shouted the umpire.

Knuckles threw again and again,
but one pitch was too low
and the other was too wide.

The count was three balls
and two strikes.

The next pitch

would decide everything.

"Come on, Harold!"

shouted Shirley on the bench.

"Keep your eye on the ball!"

shouted Big Leon.

"Make him put it where you want it!"
shouted the rest of the team,
and Mr. Lombardo looked
as if he was praying.

The ball floated towards the plate.

It was Knuckles Smith's slow ball,

his change of pace,

which always fooled batters.

Harold closed his eyes
and swung with all his might,
and—POW!—he connected!

The ball was going, going, gone
over the fence for a home run.
Harold ran around the bases,
from first to second,
from second to third.

He crossed home plate and
his teammates picked him up
and carried him on their shoulders.

"Harold, you may be
the littlest leaguer, but today
you were the biggest leaguer
of them all," said Mr. Lombardo.
And even Big Leon was cheering.